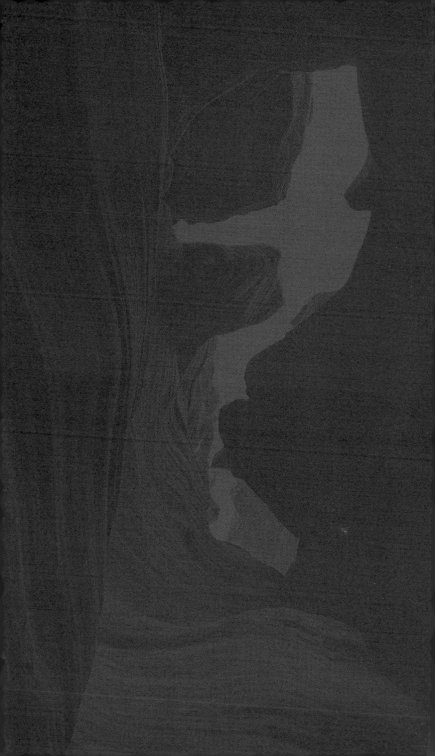

영감과 섬광 *Inspiration and Flash*

영감과 섬광

2024년 6월 10일 초판 1쇄 인쇄
2024년 6월 18일 초판 1쇄 발행

지은이 | 김종회
펴낸이 | 孫貞順

펴낸곳 | 도서출판 작가
　　　　(03756) 서울 서대문구 북아현로6길 50
　　　　전화 | 02)365-8111~2　팩스 | 02)365-8110
　　　　이메일 | cultura@cultura.co.kr
　　　　홈페이지 | www.cultura.co.kr
　　　　등록번호 | 제13-630호(2000. 2. 9.)

편집 | 손희 양진호 설재원
디자인 | 오경은 박근영
마케팅 | 박영민
관리 | 이용승

ISBN 979-11-90566-87-2 03810

값 15,000원

한국디카시 대표시선

14

김종회 디카시집

영감과 섬광

Inspiration and Flash

작가

새로운 한류 문예 장르 디카시가 발원 20주년에 이르는 뜻 깊은 해에, 네 번째 디카시집을 내놓는다. 순간 포착의 영상과 촌철살인의 시어를 결합하고, SNS를 통해 실시간으로 소통하는 디카시는 이제 하나의 대세요 시대정신이 되었다. 지금까지 국내 주요 지자체 12곳과 해외 주요 국가 및 도시 18곳에 지부가 창립되어 활동하고 있는 것이 그 증거다.

20년 성년에 이르도록 디카시 운동에 합류한 시인들이, 함께 가꾸고 가다듬은 디카시 창작의 금언이라 할 언술들을 열거해 보면 다음과 같다.

1. 디카시는 영상문화 시대로 이행된 상황을, 최적화하여 수용하는 창작 방식이다.
2. 디카시는 일상의 예술이요 예술이 일상이 되는, '생활문학'이다.
3. 디카시는 시가 아니다. 디카시는 디카시다.
4. 디카시 문예 운동은, '운동'이 아니라 '문예'가 되어야 한다.
5. 디카시인은 '동호인'의 차원을 넘어 진정한 '시인'을 지향해야 한다.

6. 디카시는 쓰기 쉬우나 잘 쓰기가 쉽지 않은 것이다.

7. 디카시의 미학적 가치, 예술성을 확보하는 것은 이 문예
   운동의 운명적 과제다.

8. 온 세계에서 한글로 쓰는 새로운 한류 문예이기에, 디카
   시는 우리의 자긍심이다.

이와 같은 절실한 방향성과 현장 철학은 내게 있어서도 언
제나 효용성 있는 창작 지침이었다. 시집의 제목을 '영감과 섬
광'이라 한 것은, 디카시가 "시인의 창작 역량과 노력에 영감靈
感을 더하고 섬광閃光의 시간이 동시에 작동하는 예술형식"이
라는 뜻이다. 이 제목은 내가 2019년 계간《디카시》여름호에
통권 30호 기념으로 쓴 축사의 제목이었다.

이 시집은 모두 5부로 구성되어 있다. 1부 〈어떤 사색과 관
찰〉은 소나기마을과 내 삶의 주변에서 특징적인 사색 및 관찰
의 장면을 포착한 것이다. 2부 〈풍경과 심경의 빛〉은 국내 여
러 지역을 여행하면서 추수한 뜻깊은 풍경과 그에 대한 심경
을 표현했다.

3부 〈미국 동남부 유적〉은 2023년 1월과 4월 두 차례에 걸쳐 워싱턴 등 동부와 댈러스 등 남부, 그리고 사우스다코다주 키스톤에 있는 마운트 러시모어의 대통령 얼굴 바위 여행 기록이다. 4부 〈미국 중서부 절경〉은 2024년 3월 LA 및 샌프란시스코와 애리조나주 내륙에 있는 엔텔롭캐년의 '생애 여행' 결과다. 말로 설명할 수 없는 자연의 신비가 거기 있었다. 5부 〈동아시아 두 여정〉은 2023년 일본 북해도와 홍콩을 방문한 날들의 소출이다.

　이렇게 모두 75편의 디카시를 하나의 시집으로 묶는 것은, 디지털카메라의 렌즈를 통해 바라본 풍광과 그 벅찬 감동을 세상의 디카시인들과 공유하기 위해서다. 이처럼 볼품 있는 책을 만들어주신 도서출판 작가에 감사드린다.

2024년 5월

김종회 시인

This year marks a meaningful milestone as it celebrates the 20th anniversary of the origin of Dicasi or Dica Poem, undeniably a new Korean literary genre. To commemorate this achievement, I hereby present my fourth Dica Poem Collection. Dica Poem is essentially defined to combine moment-capturing images and witty poetic dictums, and communicates in real time through social media. Dica Poem has now become a major trend not only domestically in Korea but also around the world. As a proof for this, the branch Dica Poem societies have so far been established and are actively involved in a variety of literary activities in eleven major local governments in Korea and seventeen major countries and cities abroad.

There are axioms for Dica Poem creation that have been cultivated and refined by poets who joined the Dica Poem Movement over the past 20 years. The statements are listed here as follows.

1. The creative method of Dica Poem is to optimize and accommodate the current situation that has moved into the era of visual culture.

2. Dica Poem is the art of everyday life, and at the same time,

it is 'living literature' where art becomes daily life.

3. Dica Poem is not a poem. Dica Poem is simply a Dica Poem.

4. Dica Poem literary movement should not be 'a movement.' It should be 'literary art.'

5. The poets of Dica Poem should aim to go beyond the level of 'an association member' and transcend into a true 'poet.'

6. Dica Poem is easy to write, but not easy to compose well.

7. The ultimate sublimation of Dica Poem is to secure aesthetic value and artistry.

8. Dica Poem is no doubt a new Korean trend of literary art written in Hangul all over the world. That is why Dica Poem is our pride.

The imminent directionality and real-life philosophy of these maxims have always been useful creative guidelines for me. I titled this poetry collection Inspiration and Flash because Dica Poem is "an art form in which inspiration is added to the poet's creative talent and effort and the flash of time works simultaneously." This title was the one I used for the speech I delivered in commemoration of the 30th issue of the 2019 quarterly summer issue of 《Dicasi》.

This poetry collection comprises five parts. Part 1 is 〈Some Thoughts and Observations〉. I captured characteristic scenes of Sonagi Village and the surroundings of my life. And the contemplation and observation are recorded in Part 1, and the ensuing Part 2 is 〈Light of Landscape and Heart〉. Here, I portrayed the meaningful scenery that I harvested while traveling to various parts of Korea and my feelings about them.

I have traveled to the eastern part of America, including Washington, to the south, Dallas, and the Presidential Face Rock of Mount Rushmore in Keystone, South Dakota, twice in January and April 2023. Part 3, entitled 〈Remains of the Southeastern United States〉," was inspired by this trip. I have also traveled to Los Angeles and San Francisco and Antelope Canyon inland Arizona in March 2024. The result of this 'trip of a lifetime' is Part 4, 〈The Scenic Views of the American Midwest〉. There I saw a mystery of nature that truly cannot be explained in words. I visited Hokkaido, Japan and Hong Kong in 2023. Part 5, 〈Two Journeys in East Asia〉 is the result of this trip.

A total of 75 Dica poems were compiled into one poetry collection. I wanted to share the scenery seen through the lens of a digital camera and its overwhelming implications with my respectful Dica poets around the world. I am grateful to the publishing company Doseo Chulpan Jakga for transforming my manuscripts into a beautiful book.

May, 2024
Written by the Poet Jong-Hoi Kim

—
차
례
—

머리말

제1부 어떤 사색과 관찰
Some Contemplation and Observation

밀어 *Sweet Words* 18

동심 놀이터 *A Childhood Playground* 20

두 겹 무지개 *Double Rainbow* 22

봄눈송이 오리 *Spring Snowflake Ducks* 24

백색 서정 *White Lyric* 26

눈의 쉼터 *Shelter of Snow* 28

사색 *Contemplation* 30

관찰 *Observation* 32

대화 *Dialogue* 34

집중 *Attentiveness* 36

한여름 밤의 꿈 *Midsummer Night Dream* 38

만첩홍도화 만개 유감 *Pity on the Full Bloom Peach Flowers* 40

방생 *Releasing* 42

자연 얼굴 *Nature Face* 44

화안花顏 *Flowery Face* 46

제2부 풍경과 심경의 빛
Scenery and Lights of the Mind

주인 없는 권좌 *No Owner on the Seat of Power* 50

직찍 청와대 *The Direct Photo Blue House* 52

경복궁의 이방인 *Foreigners in Kyungbok Palace* 54

임인년 첫 동해 바다 *The Year Imin's First East Sea* 56

동해시 능파대 촛대바위 *Donghae City Neungpade Candlestick Rock* 58

솔뫼성지 소나무떼 *The Solmoe Holy Site Pine Tree Herd* 60

솔뫼 대성전 *Solmoe Shrine* 62

의암 *Euiam* 64

충절 *Loyalty* 66

머나먼 북녘땅 *Far Distant North Side Ground* 68

울릉도 마가목 *Ulleung Island Mountain Ash* 70

울릉도 호박 *Ulleungdo Pumpkin* 72

반분 *Halving* 74

관음도 앞바다 *The Sea off Qwaneum Island* 76

새벽 바다 *The Sea at Dawn* 78

제3부 미국 동남부 유적
Historical Relics South Eastern Part of America

링컨기념관에서 의사당까지 *From Lincoln Memorial to the Capitol* 82

레오나르도 다빈치의 인물화 *Leonardo da Vinci's Portrait* 84

미국 국립미술관의 비너스 *Venus in the US National Gallery of Art* 86

스미스소니언 자연사박물관
　　　Smithsonian Museum of Natural History 88

전설의 사랑 *Legendary Love* 90

한국전쟁 희생자 추모공원 *Korean War Veterans Memorial Park* 92

베트남전쟁 희생자 추모공원 *Vietnam Veterans Memorial Park* 94

미조리 램버츠 카페 *Lambert's Cafe Missouri* 96

오클라호마 허리케인 구름 *Hurricane Cloud Oklahoma* 98

세기의 장소 *The Place of the Century* 100

묘지 지킴이 조선 유생 *Joseon Confucian Tomb Guardians* 102

눈밭 생존 나들이 *Snow Field Survival Outing* 104

5인 10장掌 *Five Persons Ten Handprints* 106

개명 *Renaming* 108

대통령들의 초상 *Presidents' Portraits* 110

원주민의 항거 *Natives' Protest* 112

미리 본 영웅 기상 *Heroic Spirit Seen Ahead* 114

제4부 미국 중서부 절경
Picturesque Scenery Midwest of America

휘장 *The Drapery* 118

불꽃 *A Flower of Fire* 120

마법사 *Magician* 122

X *X* 124

짐승들 *The Beasts* 126

곰 *A Bear* 128

계단 *The Stairs* 130

엿보기 *Peeping* 132

날개 *The Wings* 134

격류 *Intense Torrent* 136

파웰호수 *Lake Powell* 138

홀스슈밴드 *Horseshoe Bend* 140

LA 천사의 도시 *LA the Angel's City* 142

미국 북가주 상공 *The Sky of Northern California USA* 144

미국 오클랜드 산야 *Mountainous Field Oakland USA* 146

어느 화장실 *A Bathroom* 148

제5부 동아시아 두 여정
Two Journeys East Asia

이토 세이의 서재 *Ito Sei's Study* 152

미우라 아야코 집필실 *Miura Ayako's Writing Room* 154

오타루 귀빈관 노송 *The Old Pine Tree in the Otaru Public Hall* 156

다다미 내실 *Tatamis Main Room* 158

젊은 산 에조 후지 *Young Mountain Ejo Huji* 160

천지간 *Between Heaven and Earth* 162

소화신산 휴화산 *Dormant Volcano Showashin Mountain* 164

삿포로 후루사토 공원 *Furusato Park Sapporo* 166

안도 다다오 정원 *Ando Tadao Garden* 168

안도 다다오 대두 불상 *The Big Head Buddha Statue Ando Tadao* 170

바다에서 본 구룡반도 *Kowloon Peninsula Seen from the Sea* 172

완차이 홍콩 도심 *Wanchai Hong Kong Downtown* 174

어떤 사색과 관찰

Some Contemplation and Observation

밀어
Sweet Words

소나기마을 소녀네가겟방 앞뜰
촘촘하게 자리 잡은 네모필라 꽃밭
저마다 은밀한 얼굴로 말을 건네네
들을 귀 있는 자만 들을 수 있는!

Sonagi Village the Girls' Storeroom front yard
Closely wrought Square Blooming flower garden
Everyone in a secret face extends the words
Only those with ears that can hear can hear!

동심 놀이터
A Childhood Playground

한낮 해가 중천을 넘어간 한나절

내 어린 마음도 저기 뛰놀고 있네

세월 흘러도 함께 묶인 시간의 사슬

At high noon the sun went over half day

Oh my childhood heart is playing frisking over there

Though ages went over the time chain tied together

두 겹 무지개
Double Rainbow

삽상한 가을날 맑은 공기 가르며
인공 소나기 분무에 무지개 두 줄
어린이는 언제나 어른의 아버지!

Crisp Autumn day clear air splitting
Artificial rainbow spray by two rows
The Child is always father of the Man!

봄눈송이 오리
Spring Snowflake Ducks

소나기마을 갈밭머리 쉼터 길

방문객이 남긴 눈송이 오리 형제

계절의 문턱 넘어 봄 마중 나들이

Sonagi Village near the reeds field on the resting trail

Visitors left behind the snow flake duck brothers

Over the season's threshold going to meet the spring on a picnic

백색 서정
White Lyric

겨울 한복판의 문학관과 소나기마을
천하를 덮은 눈이 여기라 예외일까
맑고 밝은 서정에 사위가 적요하다
이 그림 어디에 아홉 살 소년 숨었다

Literature Hall and Sonagi Village in mid winter
Would the whole world covering snow save here
In the clear bright lyric all around is still and lonesome
In this drawing somewhere a nine-year-old boy hid

눈의 쉼터
Shelter of Snow

소나기마을 쪽빛구름 쉼터

관람객 자취 없고 얕게 눈만 쌓였다

이 풍경 '백의 연인' 그 이름을 닮았다

Sonagi Village Indigo Cloud Shelter

No traces of visitors only thinly piled up snows

This scenery 'The Sweetheart of White Robe' that name

took after

사색
Contemplation

물이 왜 물인지 물빛이 무엇인지
제 안의 소우주로 가늠하는 순간
아하! 세상이 모두 숨을 죽였구나

Water why is it water and the water color what is it
By the little universe within at the moment of guessing
Ah ha! The world stopped its breath that's it

관찰

Observation

코너 진열장 딱 내 스타일로 채웠네

풍요 속의 빈곤이라더니

오래 찾는 최애 과자 그 하나만 없네

The corner display shelves filled up right for my style

Who said poverty in affluence

Long sought my best sweets only that not seen here

대화
Dialogue

모색이 짙어가는 가을날 한나절
아이와 강아지 서로 마음 나눈다
바탕이 순수하면 모든 말 통한다

Shades of evening getting thicker in the autumn half day
A child and a puppy share their minds between them
If the basis pure all words get through

집중
Attentiveness

두 눈의 초점이 모인 응시

생명은 모두 근본이 닮았나니

아이도 어린 짐승도 서로 궁금해

Two eyes focused together on contemplation

For all breathing lives resembled the foundation just like that

A child also wonders about a little beast between them

한여름 밤의 꿈
Midsummer Night Dream

산속 휴양지를 밝히는 오색 불빛

여기 동화의 나라라 불러도 될까

아니지! 풍경보다 먼저 마음인 것을

A mountain resort brightening five color lights

Can this place be called a country of fairy tale

Oh no! Mind comes first not the scenery

만첩홍도화 만개 유감
Pity on the Full Bloom Peach Flowers

이미 봄이 깊어 천하 초목심인데

무엇이 그리도 급했을까

가지 뻗을 사이도 없이 몸체에 겹꽃을

Spring already deepened with thick vegetation all under heaven

For what were they with such a haste

For boughs no time to reach out on their body the multi-layered flowers

방생
Releasing

네 해 가깝도록 앞마당 연못에 있던 생명
아침저녁으로 돌보던 금잉어 세 마리
북한강으로 보내며 이렇게 미어지는 가슴

Almost four years long in the pond at the front yard the lives
Mornings and evenings looked after three golden carp
Into Bukhan River being sent with heart torn like this

자연 얼굴
Nature Face

작은 바위 중동을 감싼

저 푸른 잎새들

날마다 보던 풍경인데

문득 오늘은 감격스럽네

Little rocks Middle East surrounding

Those green leaves

Everyday would look at the scenery though

Unexpectedly today so impressive

화안花顏
Flowery Face

꽃잎 하나에서 청양靑陽의 봄을

나뭇잎 한 장에서 조락凋落의 가을을

여기 국화 운집하니 계절의 향연饗宴

In one flower leaf all the bright light spring

In one sheet of tree leaf wilting and falling autumn

Here the chrysanthemum in crowd and the season's

banquet

제2부

풍경과 심경의 빛

Scenery and Lights
of the Mind

주인 없는 권좌

No Owner on the Seat of Power

한때 서슬 푸른 별의 자리였건만

화무십일홍에 또 권불십년이라

필부 곧은 심사로 부러울 바 없으리

Once used to be one for the star with mighty power but

No flowers last red ten days nor does the highest power for
ten years

This humble man won't envy that with straight thinking in
mind

직찍 청와대
The Direct Photo Blue House

경복궁 짓고 남은 자투리땅에
푸른색 기와로 현대사의 기록을
아무렴! 빛과 그늘 동반하며 썼구나

Kyungbok Palace built on the little piece of land left
With blue color roof tiles recording the history of modern
days
Certainly! Written accompanying lights and shades

경복궁의 이방인
Foreigners in Kyungbok Palace

먼바다 건너온 우리 고궁의 손님

한복 차려입는 법은 어떻게 알고

동서 융합으로 일상 속에 내렸네

The far sea beyond came these quests to our old palace

Hanbok attire dressed up in the methods how did they know

By East west fusion into daily lives descended

임인년 첫 동해 바다
The Year Imin's First East Sea

새 아침 이름 붙여 그윽히 바라보니

인류 문화사 소거와 재생 거기 다 있네

늘 만나던 바다 또한 눈과 뜻에 달렸느니

The new morning named and looked in a quiet heart

The mankind cultural history deleted and revived exists there

The sea always seen also depended on the eyes and
intention

동해시 능파대 촛대바위
Donghae City Neungpade Candlestick Rock

장구한 시간 파도가 깎은 석회암

석림의 선두 암석 기둥 촛대바위

하늘도 바다도 아무 말이 없는데

여기 잠긴 세월 그 누가 짐작할까

Eternal time the waves carved the limestone

The Rock forest leading stone pillar a candlestick rock

The sky nor the sea has any words

Here submerged ages who can ever calculate

솔뫼성지 소나무떼
The Solmoe Holy Site Pine Tree Herd

김대건 신부 탄생지를 이른 말
왜 솔뫼라 했는지 저절로 알겠네
믿음 위해 목숨 던진 귀한 희생
2백 년 세월 옛터에 청청한 적송

The words known as Father Kim Dae Geon's birthplace

Why called Solmoe naturally understood

For faith cast his life rare sacrifice

On the old days' site aged 200 years the fresh green red
pine trees

솔뫼 대성전
Solmoe Shrine

한낮인데도 성자들의 형용 휘황하다
생전 이타행으로 모두 내어주었으니
그 광영 시공을 넘어 사뭇 밝히 빛나다

Even in the midday the saints' figures brilliant

For their whole lives for altruism all taken out and given

Their brilliant honors beyond time and space quite

shine

의암

Euiam

논개 사당에서 내려다보는 남강

고즈넉한 강심에 순국의 둥근 바위

후세에 누가 있어 이 역사 이어 가랴

From the Nongae Shrine looking down at River Nam

In the lonely river heart the patriotic round rock

Who in the future generations will this history keep

handing down

충절
Loyalty

진주성을 침범한 왜군 장수 끌어안고
두 손깍지로 남강에 몸을 던진 의기
그 숭고한 자태 이당 김은호가 그렸네

The Jinju fortress invading Japanese Woe pirate general
she embraced
    With her two hands folded tight and threw her body the
righteous woman
    Her sublime appearance Lee Dang Gim Eun Ho drew

머나먼 북녘땅
Far Distant North Side Ground

강화도 양사면 평화전망대

임진강 너머 북한 땅 아련하네

한눈에 지척인데 80년 세월이라니

이산의 눈물로 이 강 마를 날 없겠네

The Gangwha Island Yangsa Myeon Peace Observation
Platform

Imjin River beyond over North Korean ground so dim

Within bare eyes' short distance yet 80 years time so
long

By tears for family separation this river drying day will
never be

울릉도 마가목

Ulleung Island Mountain Ash

겉보기에 전혀 다를 것 없는 보통 나무

온갖 약재 효험으로 의서에 기록이라니

아서라! 또 가공된 건강 약품 사고 말았네

Seemingly no different at all just ordinary trees

All kinds of medicinal effectiveness read the medicinal
books

Stop! Again ended up buying the processed health
medicinal products

울릉도 호박
Ulleungdo Pumpkin

호박엿의 본고장 뜰에 쌓인 원재료

여름 햇볕과 가을바람으로 영글었네

저마다 삶의 길 만상도처 유청산이라

Pumpkin taffy native home yard piled up raw material

By summer sunlight and autumn wind ripened solid

Respectively on the way of life all things have their places

to rest

반분
Halving

여기 오직 하늘과 바다밖에 없는 곳
온 세상 절반씩 가진 일도양단의 도식
내 삶의 이분법은 이득인가 실책인가

Here a place of only the sky and the sea and nothing else

All the world each has half figure by one sword stroke
into two

The dichotomy of my life a benefit or an error

관음도 앞바다
The Sea off Qwaneum Island

참 맑고 푸른 빛

사람 손으로 꾸밀 수 없는 청량

바닷가에 숨죽인 별유천지 비인간

Truly clear blue light

By people's hands not creatable clear and clean

By the sea another inhuman world of breath taking

quietness

새벽 바다

The Sea at Dawn

동터 오는 바다 저편에 새벽 여명
울릉도 도동의 아침은 무얼 준비할까
되새긴 생각의 크기 배 한 척만 못하네

The day breaking sea beyond the dawn twilight
Ulleung Island Dodong morning what does it prepare
Oh my contemplated idea size no bigger than a boat

제3부

미국 동남부 유적

Historical Relics South
Eastern Part of America

링컨기념관에서 의사당까지
From Lincoln Memorial to the Capitol

한눈에 보이는 이 역사의 공간에

장엄한 오벨리스크 기개가 오연

이 정치 역정 몰라도 행복한 서민들

At a glance seen the historical space

Majestic obelisk with its haughty pride

Happy public even unaware of this historical path

레오나르도 다빈치의 인물화
Leonardo da Vinci's Portrait

평생 네 점을 그린 그의 초상화 중에
초장에 그린 17세 소녀의 청초
미국 국립미술관 최고의 자랑이라네
입가에 미소만 더하면 거의 모나리자라

In his lifetime painted four pieces of portraits

The first piece a 17-year-old girl drawn pure beauty

Called the US National Gallery of Art's highest pride

Only a smile added around her mouth almost Mona Lisa

미국 국립미술관의 비너스
Venus in the US National Gallery of Art

백수의 왕 사자를 이불처럼 깔고서
고개 돌려 무엇을 보고 있을까
이 모양이면 세상 모든 남자는
여성의 미색 앞에 살았다 할 것 없으리

King of beasts the lion underlain like a quilt

What is she looking at with her head turned over

With this appearance all men around the world

May be unable to say they ever lived before the beauty of a

woman

스미스소니언 자연사박물관
Smithsonian Museum of Natural History

출입 현관에 육중한 코끼리 박제

위층에는 세기의 보석과 미이라실

어쩌면 코끼리가 사람 구경하는 듯

In the parlor at the entrance door a massive stuffed
elephant

On the upper floor the rooms for the jewels of the
century and mummies

Perhaps the elephant has a sightseeing on people looks
like it

전설의 사랑
Legendary Love

달빛이 비칠 때면 애너벨 리의 꿈이

별빛이 떠오를 때 그 빛나는 눈동자가

마침내 에드거 앨런 포를 잠재운 자리

Every time the moonlight shined Annabel Lee's dream

When the starlight rose up that shining pupil

At last put Edgar Allan Poe to sleep here

한국전쟁 희생자 추모공원
Korean War Veterans Memorial Park

16개국 숱한 생명의 대가를 치르고
8만 리 먼 땅 한국의 자유를 얻었으니
이 공원 세운 윌리엄 웨버도 거기 함께

At the cost of a lot of lives from sixteen nations
80 thousand ri distant land Korea freedom earned
William Weber who erected this park included there too

베트남전쟁 희생자 추모공원
Vietnam Veterans Memorial Park

삶에서 죽음으로 가는 일직선의 길

그 선두에 섰던 젊은 생령들

이제는 그저 이름 몇 자로 남았으니

신이여 이 문제의 정답은 어디 있나요

The way of a straight line going from life to death

The young people who stood in front

Ended up now being left in the name of just a few words

Please God where the correct answer is

미조리 렘버츠 카페
Lambert's Cafe Missouri

미국 전역에 알려진 관광명소 서민 식당

값싸고 푸짐하고 맛있는 여행자 쉼터

따뜻한 실용주의와 자유로운 정신의 조화

Throughout American well-known tourist attraction for

general people's restaurant

Reasonable abundant delicious tourists' resting place

Warm practicalism and free spirit in harmony

오클라호마 허리케인 구름
Hurricane Cloud Oklahoma

텍사스로 내려가는 69번 하이웨이

차창 밖으로 장쾌한 구름 기둥이 섰다

폭풍 모형이나 부드럽기는 솜사탕이다

Highway 69 going down to Texas

Outside the car window a thrilling cloud pillar stood up

The storm figure though is the softness cotton candy

세기의 장소
The Place of the Century

1963년 케네디 대통령 암살 현장

길바닥엔 흰색 엑스 표시만 남고

저격한 곳 6층 건물은 그대로인데

후인 몇몇 회상에 잠겨 발길 머무네

The spot President Kennedy assassinated 1963

On the road surface left only the X mark

The six story sniping building as it was

Some of the later persons stay lost in recollection

묘지 지킴이 조선 유생
Joseon Confucian Tomb Guardians

댈러스 예술의 거리 중간 어름에
8만 리 바다 건너고 대륙을 종단해 온
조선의 묘지 석상 두 기가 서 있다
안내자는 이 도시 첫 이민자라 말한다

In the middle junction of Dallas street of art

The 80 thousand ri sea crossed over and ran through the

continent to arrive

The Joseon's two tomb stone figures standing up

The guide says the first immigrants to this city

눈밭 생존 나들이
Snow Field Survival Outing

미국 사우스다코타주 키스톤

산장 인근 숲길에 사슴 한 가족

젖은 땅 어딘가에 양식 있을까

선한 눈길 들어 찾고 또 찾는데

Keystone South Dakota US

Near the mountain cottage on the forest trail a family of deer

Will there somewhere wet be food

Raising their kind eyesights looking out again and again ever

5인 10장掌
Five Persons Ten Handprints

눈 내린 베란다 탁상에 마음 모으기

5인의 장인掌印 10개의 수적手跡

때아닌 4월 적설이 행위예술 도왔네

On the snowed veranda table the minds gathered

Five persons' hand stamps and ten hand traces

Untimely April snow accumulation helped the

performance art

개명
Renaming

블랙 힐에서 마운트 러시모어로

형용을 바꾸며 명호까지 바꾸었네

신의 창조 영역에 인간의 발을 디밀고

From Black Hill into Mount Rushmore

Changed the figure and changed the name title too

In the realm of God's creation pushing in humans' feet

대통령들의 초상
Presidents' Portraits

마운트 러시모어 놀라운 풍광

워싱턴 제퍼슨 루스벨트 링컨

존경할 줄 알아야만 존경 받느니

Mount Rushmore surprising scene

Washington Jefferson Roosevelt Lincoln

Must know how to respect to be respected

원주민의 항거
Natives' Protest

점령자 국가에 바위산 조각 도전장

인디언 영웅 크레이지 호스의 기마상

존경의 대상에 인종차별 철폐하라!

한 지역에서 백 년 앞 보며 한 땀 한 땀

Against the occupants' nation the rock mountain
carving challenge

Indian hero Crazy Horse's horse riding statue

Abolish the racial discrimination against the object of
respect!

One stitch again and again seeing one hundred years
ahead in one territory

미리 본 영웅 기상
Heroic Spirit Seen Ahead

크레이지 호스 마운틴이 건너다 보이는
기념센터 마당에 미래 완성형 조형 있다
비로소 저 산이 어떻게 조각될지 말한다
은백색 색감으로 종내 백마 탄 장군이다

Crazy Horse Mountain seen yonder

From the memorial center yard located a sculpture yet

to be perfected

Telling eventually how that mountain will look carved

In a silver white color tone a white horse back riding general

제4부

미국 중서부 절경

Picturesque Scenery
Midwest of America

휘장
The Drapery

애리조나 앤텔롭캐년

사암과 물과 빛의 조화

천고의 세월 기다려

여기 휘장을 열었네

Arizona Antelope Canyon

Harmony of sandstone and water and light

Waiting ages of eternity and

Here opened the drapery

불꽃
A Flower of Fire

동굴 끝 햇빛은 불타는 날개
이 질곡 벗어나면 창공이리니
오르막 힘들어도 마침내 갈 길

The sunlight at the end of the cave is the burning wing
If breaking away this yoke surely will there be a blue sky
Challenging as the uphill is it is a way to go eventually

마법사
Magician

저 어둠 속 어디에 숨어있나

세상을 바꾸는 마법의 램프

흑암 속에서 찾은 사랑의 심장

Inside that darkness where is it hidden

The world changing magic lamp

From the sheer darkness found the heart of love

X
X

엔텔롭캐년 천정의 하늘

X자 모양이라 계곡 이름 되었네

사암 벽과 하늘이 서로 손잡고

The ceiling's sky of Antelope Canyon

Shaped like the letter X thereby became the valley name

The sandstone wall and the sky hand in hand

짐승들
The Beasts

지저地底에 웅크린 짐승의 형상

오랜 갈구와 욕망에 주린 영혼

내 안에는 저 절박한 모습 없을까

In the depths of the earth crouched beast figures

Longtime longing and desires starving souls

Within me won't there that desperateness

곰
A Bear

피라미드도 아닌데 이집트 문양

인고의 세월 지킨 웅녀의 몸짓

동서고금을 막론하고 곰은 동굴 속에

Not a pyramid but Egyptian patterns

Woong-nyeo's posture keeping the years of endurance

All around East and West timelessly bears inside the cave

계단
The Stairs

그대 보았는가 천국으로 가는 계단
돌 하나하나마다 사연이 묻혔나니
이윽고 저 높이에 닿아야 되돌아볼 터

Did thou ever see the stairs going to heavens

Because in each stone one by one has a story buried

After having to reach that height then only will look
back

엿보기
Peeping

검은 벽을 가림막으로 얼굴 내밀어

저 멀리 단단한 주광晝光을 바라보네

작아야 선명함을 이제 비로소 알았다니

Showing the face through the black wall of a tormentor

Looking at that distant solid daylight

Not until now did I know that it should be small to be clear

날개
The Wings

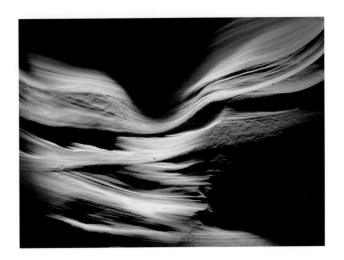

모래 바위 적층이 쌓아온 광휘

어둠을 타고 넘는 천사의 날개

내 작은 소망도 거기 함께 싣고자

The stacking layers on the sandy rocks piled up the
brilliance

An angel's wing riding on the darkness and going beyond

Wishing to load even my small desires on it

격류
Intense Torrent

빛의 흐름이 이토록 격렬하다니!

암반의 표정에도 휘모리장단 있었네

숨은 열정으로 저 높은 곳을 향한 용틀임

The stream of light how could it be this intense

Even on the rock base looks had been whimori the
rhythm

With hidden passion the forceful belch toward that high
place

파월호수
Lake Powell

유타와 애리조나주에 걸친

글렌캐년의 광활한 인공 호수

나바호 네이션의 젖줄

삶의 모든 풍광 물속에 담았네

Bordering Utah and Arizona

Glen Canyon's infinitely spacious man-made lake

Navaho Nation's life line

All scenery of lives placed on the water

홀스슈밴드
Horseshoe Bend

페이지 시가 교외의 콜로라도강

말발굽 형용으로 깊이 발을 담갔네

누가 있어 저 오랜 사연 풀어 말할까

Colorado River on the outskirts of City of Page

The horseshoe figure deeply dipped its feet

Who there can talk the interpretation of that long story

LA 천사의 도시
LA the Angel's City

사막 땅을 도회로 만든 역사役事

그 조화는 천사의 것인가

산과 바다의 아름다움 굽어보며

마음 편지 한 장 나성羅城에 두었네

The history of making the desert into a city

Is the harmony the angel's

Looking down at the beauty of the mountains and rivers

Left a mindful letter in LA

미국 북가주 상공
The Sky of Northern California USA

이 튼튼한 날개로 하늘 가르고

저 넓은 지평 오시傲視하듯 내려다보니

인간 만사 모두가 몇 알 좁쌀만 같네

By this stout wings splitting the sky

Looking down at that wide ground like arrogantly

Human matters all like some hulled millet

미국 오클랜드 산야
Mountainous Field Oakland USA

겨울철 우기 지나 새봄 맞으니

황토색 산허리에 연초록 치맛자락

평온한 언덕 기슭 마음 두기 한가롭네

New Spring arriving past the rainy winter season

At the ocher mountainside a part of light yellow skirt

Leisurely leave the mind on the peaceful bank of the hill

어느 화장실
A Bathroom

일상의 예술이자 예술의 일상

자기 영역에 대한 극한 집중

그 연출로 조형된 유다른 공간

This is an art of daily life and a daily life of art as well

Extreme concentration on his area

By that performance unusual space formed

이토 세이의 서재
Ito Sei's Study

북해도 오타루의 시립박물관
여러 문인 한데 모인 전시관 한편에
전 일본에 문명 높은 문인의 창작실
이 책들은 무엇을 기억하고 있을까

Municipal Museum Otaru Hokkaido

In the one exhibition hall room several literary men
gathered

A writing room for literary men with high fame over
entire Japan

What would these books remember

미우라 아야코 집필실
Miura Ayako's Writing Room

『빙점』으로 히로인이 된 세기의 작가

병마와 싸우며 이웃 배려한 고운 마음

소박한 이 집필실 넘어 일본으로 세계로

By *Bing Jeom* became a heroine the writer of the century

Fighting the evil disease had gracious mind considerate
to the neighbors

Beyond this humble place over Japan and over the world

오타루 귀빈관 노송
The Old Pine Tree in the Otaru Public Hall

105년 전에 짓기 시작한 부호의 고택

국가 지정 역사적 건축물 제3호

건물보다 더 고색창연한 노송의 의연

The old house by a rich man started building 105 years

ago

Nation designated historical building no.3

The resolute old pine looking older than the building

다다미 내실
Tatamis Main Room

정갈한 숨결 살아 있는 적막한 공간

100년간 이 자리를 거쳐 간 사람들

누가 일러 이를 전통문화라 했을까

Lonely Space Clean Breath Alive

In the time span of 100 years inhabited people

Who told this is a traditional culture

젊은 산 에조 후지
Young Mountain Ejo Huji

윌리엄 클라크 농촌 선교사가

저 산을 보고 청년이여 야망을!

산정은 구름을 이고 말이 없는데

William Clark the farm village missionary

Looking at that mountain Boys be ambitious!

The mountain head carrying the cloud has no words

though

천지간
Between Heaven and Earth

북해도 내륙을 점령한 도야호 풍랑

하늘과 섬과 물이 조화롭게 만나다

사방 천지에 인간의 힘은 미약하다

Windy water waves at Doya Lake inland Hokkaido

The sky the island the water meet in harmony

In all directions heaven and earth human power is feeble

소화신산 휴화산
Dormant Volcano Showashin Mountain

여러 차례 분화를 거쳐

2000년에 마지막 불을 뿜은 화산

불과 20여 년 전인데

외양 형상은 수염 있는 번개 신 얼굴

그 속에 아직도 용암 들끓고 있다는데

Through several times of eruption

Belched forth the last fire in the year 2000

Not any longer than 20 years or so ago though

Outward looks like the lightning god's face with beard

The inside is said still seething with lava though

삿포로 후루사토 공원
Furusato Park Sapporo

칠레 이스터섬의 바빌론 석상을 모방한

대형 인물 조각의 행렬이 사뭇 장대하네

이 흉내 내기를 언제까지 답습할까

Imitating Babylon Stone Statues Easter Island Chile

The parade of large human sculptures is quite grand

Until when will they repeat this mimicking

안도 다다오 정원
Ando Tadao Garden

마음을 비추는 명경이 넓고 고요하다
물의 정원이 빛나는 건축인 이유다
빛과 물과 자연을 재구성한 공간 철학자

The polished mirror reflecting the mind is wide and quiet
That is why the water garden is a light shining architecture
The light and water and nature recomposed space
philosopher

안도 다다오 대두 불상
The Big Head Buddha Statue Ando Tadao

밖에서 보면 큰 머리만 보이고

안에서 보면 노천 하늘이 광원이라

부처를 자연으로 이끈 순후한 상상력

If looked from outside only the head is seen

If looked from inside it is the light source uncovered all

the way

The Buddha to nature is led by warm-hearted imagination

바다에서 본 구룡반도
Kowloon Peninsula Seen from the Sea

땅끝 물 끝을 모두 빌딩으로 채우고
도회의 울밀한 그림과 촘촘한 랜드마크
그 가운데 인간사의 모든 형용 숨었으리

Filling the land and water to their ends with buildings
The city's dense and compact drawing and close landmarks
Among them surely hidden are all the human stories

완차이 홍콩 도심
Wanchai Hong Kong Downtown

옥상 정원이 있고서도 저 높은 마천루

땅 좁고 사람 넘치는 곳의 운명적 형상

멀리 뵈는 바다조차 그 풍경에 갇혀 있네

That high skyscrapers even above the roof garden

A fateful image of the place for narrow land with
overflowing population

Even the sea seen afar is locked by the scenery

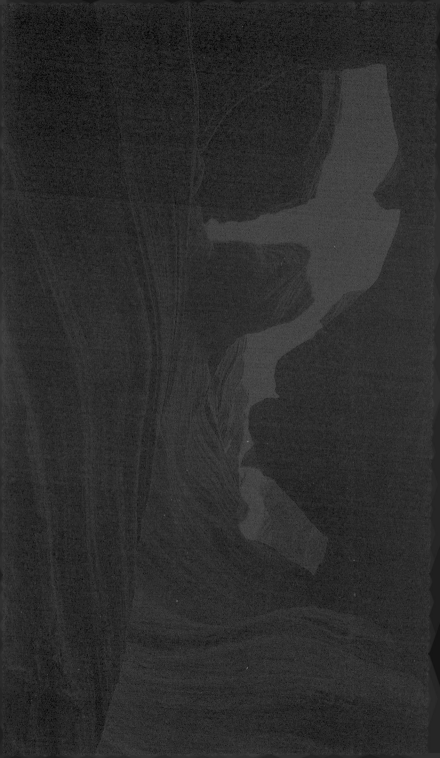